THE TRUTH ABOUT
Easter
RABBITS

THE · TRUTH · ABOUT
Easter Rabbits

COMPILED BY BLUE LANTERN STUDIO

MMVI

GREEN TIGER PRESS

COPYRIGHT © 2005, BLUE LANTERN STUDIO

ISBN 1-59583-011-1

ISBN13 978-1-59583-011-1

SECOND PRINTING PRINTED IN CHINA THROUGH COLORCRAFT LTD., HONG KONG ALL RIGHTS RESERVED

GREEN TIGER PRESS
A DIVISION OF LAUGHING ELEPHANT BOOKS

3645 INTERLAKE AVENUE NORTH SEATTLE, WASHINGTON 98103

WWW.LAUGHINGELEPHANT.COM

There is not
just one Easter Rabbit,
but many Easter Rabbits!

They live all over the world.

They are different sizes, different colors,
and do different things the rest of the year
to support themselves and their families.

The one thing they all have in common is their
dedication to celebrating Easter by decorating
eggs beautifully, and then delivering them
as gifts to the world's children.

In this book I will introduce you to a few
Easter Rabbits, and show you how
they do their work.

Clyde Bunn, an English rabbit, is a doctor.

Ernesto is a professional juggler who makes a living entertaining in parks.

Jeanette is a milliner who sells hats to fine lady rabbits.

The Johnson family, from Iowa, love baseball,
and field an excellent family team.

Ian sings in his church
choir, with a beautiful
tenor voice.

Tio, from Chile, is an
enthusiastic gardener.
He starts the day by
delivering flowers to
neighbors and friends.

Easter Rabbits enjoy life, each in their own way, just as we do. The young ones love to play at dressing up, and egg jumping is popular almost everywhere.

Many enjoy shopping.

The young ones go to school,
and prepare themselves for adult responsibilities.

Many rabbits are musical, such as Fritz and Hans,
who perform at every possible opportunity.

Everyone shares in the work that needs to be done.

When they are old enough, they have dates, so they can get to know other rabbits and choose a husband or wife.

Then they marry and raise families.

There are many large and happy Easter Rabbit families.

They enjoy fine summer weather outdoors.

And Easter Rabbit children have fun in the snow,
as human children do.

When the Easter season draws near all Easter Rabbits
feel a mounting excitement.

Each plans what gifts he will prepare, and eagerly starts
thinking of the ways in which the eggs will be decorated.

They buy the necessary supplies.

The dyeing of eggs is an exciting time for all the family.

The colors are often made from plants,
and roots, and flowers.

Many of the eggs are brightly painted.

Designs are often added.

This requires care and planning, but the results are worth the work.

Everyone helps, but even so there are so many eggs to be prepared that the work goes on late into the night.

On the night before Easter Sunday the egg deliveries
start before the sun rises.

Most Easter Rabbits
carry the eggs in packs
or baskets.

In the lake country of
Canada a boat is necessary.

A Bicycle is a great help in
the mountains of Austria.

In the vastness of the Russian steppes railroad trains are used.

Cuban Rabbits often use old-fashioned automobiles to cover their rounds.

Massive eggshells can be used in emergencies, as boats.

In Peru eggs are delivered to isolated mountain towns by cannon.

In towns walking is the simplest and best way to deliver the eggs.

Irish rabbits employ carts drawn by chickens.

Usually the eggs are delivered secretly.

The rising sun is the only one who catches a glimpse of most Easter Rabbits.

Sometimes, however, they are caught delivering the eggs.

The child who sees this usually screams in surprise and
delight. And the Easter Rabbit is startled too.

Sometimes the meetings are calm.

Any boy or girl who does surprise an Easter Rabbit is very lucky, for it turns out to be a wonderful experience.

Frequently they stay and enjoy the day
with their new friends.

Everyone shares in the joy of a wonderful Easter.

When the young rabbits finally go home, they find that
their mothers have saved them eggs to enjoy.

The young rabbits return to school and learning.

They resume their happy everyday lives.

They all look forward to the wonderful year ahead, and
the rabbit children especially to Christmas.

Now that the excitement of Easter is over
the rabbits relax.

They remember, with great joy, the many beautiful eggs,
and all the happy children ...

... and they dream of Easters to come.